The Little Prince

By
Antoine de Saint-Exupéry

SANAGE
PUBLISHING HOUSE

Paperback: 978-811900701-1

Printed by: Manipal Technologies Limited, Manipal

Sanage Publishing House LLP
Mumbai, India

sanagepublishing@gmail.com

Antoine de Saint-Exupéry (29 June 1900 – 31 July 1944), was a French writer and Poet. He is best remembered for his novella The Little Prince (Le Petit Prince) and for his lyrical aviation writings, including Wind, Sand and Stars and Night Flight. He became a laureate of several of France's highest literary awards and also won the United States National Book Award in 1939.He began writing the Little Prince during World War II, after Germany's invasion of France had forced him to give up aviation and flee to New York. in addition to his torturous thoughts of the war in Europe, having to leave his homeland and no longer being able to fly planes affected him deeply. the novel's nostalgia for childhood indicates both Saint-Exupéry's homesick desire to return to France and his hope of returning to a time of peace.

CONTENTS

TO LEON WERTH

I apologize to the children for dedicating this book to a grown-up. I have a good excuse: this grown-up is the best friend I have in the world. I have another good excuse: this grown-up can understand everything, even children's books. I have a third good excuse: this grown-up lives in France where he is hungry and cold. He needs to be comforted. If all these excuses are not enough, I will then dedicate this book to the child who became that grown-up. All grown-ups were first children. (But few of them remember it.) So, I correct my dedication:

To Leon Werth

when he was a little boy.

I

When I was six years old, I once saw a magnificent picture in a book on the virgin forest called Stories of Life. It was a boa constrictor that had swallowed a wild beast. Here is a copy of the drawing.

It was written in the book; Boa constrictors swallow their whole prey without chewing.

Then they cannot move, and they sleep during the six months of their digestion.

I then thought a lot about the adventures of the jungle and, in turn, succeeded, with a colored pencil, in drawing my very first drawing. It was like this:

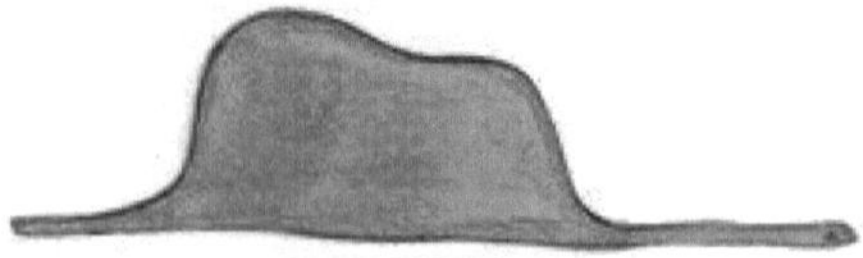

I showed my masterpiece to the grown-ups and asked them if my drawing frightened them.

They said, Why would a hat be scary?

My drawing was not of a hat. It was a boa constrictor digesting an elephant. I then drew the inside of the boa constrictor, so that the grown-ups could understand. They always required more explanation. My second drawing was like this:

The grown-ups advised me to leave aside the drawings of boa constrictors from the outside or the inside, and to interest myself instead in geography, history, calculation, and grammar. Thus, at the age of six, I abandoned a magnificent career as a painter. I had been discouraged by the failure of my first drawing and my second drawing. Grown-ups never understand anything on their own, and it is tiring for children to always have to give them explanations.

So, I had to choose another profession. I learned to fly planes. I flew all over the world.

And geography, that's right, served me well. I knew how to recognize, at first glance,

China, or Arizona. It is useful if you have gone astray during the night.

I have had, in the course of my life, a lot of contact with many serious people. I have lived among the grown-ups. I saw them up close. It did not really improve my opinion of them.

When I met one that seemed to me a little lucid, I had them experience my drawing number 1, which I had preserved. I wanted to know if they could come to a real understanding. But they always replied: It's a hat. After that I spoke to them neither of boa constrictors, nor of virgin forests, nor of stars. I put myself within their reach. I talked about bridge, golf, politics, and ties. And the grown-ups were glad to know such a reasonable man.

II

So, I lived alone, with no one to talk to, until a breakdown in the Sahara desert six years ago. Something had broken in my engine. And since I had neither a mechanic nor a passenger with me, I prepared to try, by myself, to make a difficult reprieve. It was a matter of life and death. I had hardly any water to drink for a week.

The first night I fell asleep on the sand a thousand miles from any inhabited land. I was much more isolated than a castaway on a raft in the middle of the ocean. Then you imagine my surprise, at dawn, when a funny little voice woke me up. She said:

" Please draw me a sheep! - Hein!

- Draw me a sheep… "

I jumped on my feet as if I had been struck by lightning. I rubbed my eyes well. I watched. And I saw a very extraordinary little man who looked at me gravely. This is the best portrait I later managed to make of him.

But my drawing, of course, is much less ravishing than the model. It is not my fault. I had been discouraged in my career as a painter by the grown-ups at the age of six, and I had learned nothing to draw, except closed boas and open boas.

I looked at this apparition with eyes full of astonishment. Do not forget that I was a thousand miles from any inhabited region. Now my little fellow seemed to me neither astray, nor dead of fatigue, nor dead of hunger, nor death of thirst, nor dead of fear. He had not the appearance of a child lost in the middle of the desert, a thousand miles from any inhabited region. When I finally succeeded in speaking, I said to him:

" What are you doing here? "

And he repeated to me, very gently, as a very serious thing:

" Please draw me a sheep… "

When the mystery is too impressive, we do not dare to disobey. As absurd as it seemed to me a thousand miles from all inhabited places and in danger of death, I took out of my pocket a sheet of paper and a pen. But I remembered that I had studied geography, history, calculation, and grammar and I told the little fellow (with a little bad humor) that I did not know how to draw. He replied,

" It does not matter. Draw me a sheep. "

As I had never drawn a sheep, I thought of him as one of the only two drawings of which I was capable. That of the boa closed. And I was astounded to hear the little fellow reply:

" No ! No ! I do not want an elephant in a boa. A boa is very dangerous, and an elephant is very cumbersome. My place is tight. I need a sheep. Draw me a sheep."

I drew. Then

He looked attentively, then:

" No! That one is already very ill. Do another one. "

I drew:

He looked attentively, then:

"No! That one is already very ill. Do another one. "

I drew:

My friend smiled gently, indulgently:

"You see … it's not a sheep, it's a ram. He has horns … "

So, I still refused my drawing:

But he was refused, like the preceding ones:

"This one is too old. I want a long-lived sheep. "

Then, for lack of patience, as I was anxious to begin the dismantling of my engine, I scribbled this drawing:

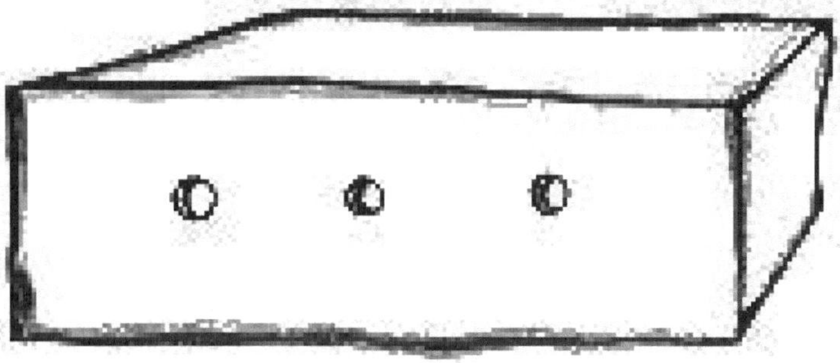

Then I threw:

"That's the box. The sheep you want is in it. "

But I was much surprised to see the face of my young judge illuminated:

"That's exactly how I wanted it!" Do you think that sheep are to be found in this country?

- Why?

- Because at home it's very small …

- Surely that will suffice. I gave you a tiny sheep. "He, leaned his head toward the drawing:

"Not so small as that. He fell asleep… "

And so, I made the acquaintance of the little prince.

III

It took me a long time to understand where he came from. The little prince, who asked me many questions, never seemed to hear mine. These are words spoken by chance that, little by little, have revealed all to me. So, when he saw my plane for the first time (I will not draw my plane, it is a drawing too complicated for me) he asked me:

"What is that thing?"

It's not a thing. It flies. It's a plane. This is my plane. "And I was proud to tell him I was flying. Then he exclaimed: "How! You have fallen from heaven!

Yes, I said modestly.

"Ah! Now that's funny… "

And the little prince had a very pretty burst of laughter, which irritated me very much. I wish to take my misfortunes seriously. Then he added:

"Then you too come from heaven!" What planet are you from?

I caught a glimpse in the mystery of his presence, and I suddenly questioned:

"So, you're from another planet?"

But he did not answer me. He nodded softly as he looked at my plane:

"It's true that you cannot come very far from it."

And he sank into a reverie that lasted for a long time. Then, taking my sheep out of his pocket, he plunged into the contemplation of his treasure.

You can imagine how intrigued I was by this half-confidence about "the other planets." I therefore endeavored to learn more:

"Where do you come from, my little fellow?" Where is "at home"? Where do you want to take my sheep?

He replied after a meditative silence:

"What is good, with the box you gave me, is that, at night, it will serve him as a house."

Of course. And if you are kind, I will also give you a rope to tie it up during the day. And a picket. "

The proposal seemed to shock the little prince:

"Attach it?" What a funny idea!

"But if you do not tie him, he'll go anywhere, and he'll get lost."

And my friend burst into laughter again:

But where do you want him to go!

Anywhere. Right in front of him... Then the little prince gravely remarked,

It does not matter, it's so small, at home!

And, with a little melancholy, perhaps, he added:

Straight ahead you cannot go far …

IV

I had learned a second very important thing: that its original planet was scarcely larger than a house!

It could not surprise me much. I knew that besides the big planets like the Earth, Jupiter, Mars, Venus, which have been given names, there are hundreds of others that are sometimes so small that it is very hard for them To see the telescope. When an astronomer discovers one of them, he names it as a number. He calls it, for example, "the asteroid 325".

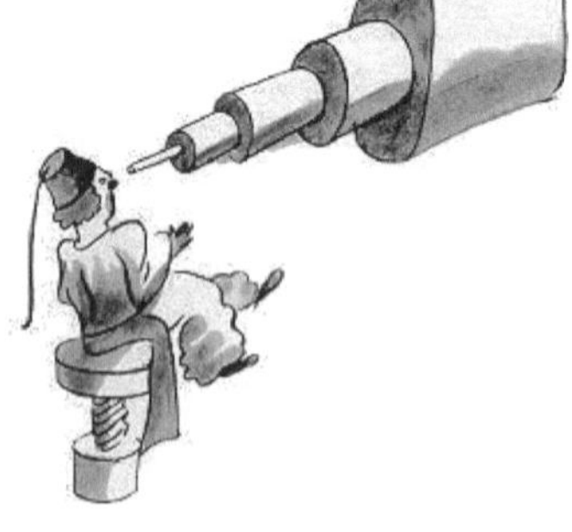

I have serious reasons to believe that the planet

from which the little prince came is the asteroid B 612. This asteroid was seen only once in 1909 by a Turkish astronomer in the telescope.

He had then made a great demonstration of his discovery at an International Astronomy Congress. But nobody believed him because of his costume. Big people are like that.Fortunately for the reputation of the asteroid B 612, a Turkish dictator imposed on his people, under penalty of death, to dress European. The astronomer resumed his demonstration in 1920, in a very elegant dress. And this time everyone was of his opinion.

If I have told you these details about the asteroid B 612 and if I have given you its number, it is because of the big people. Big people like the numbers. When you tell them about a new friend, they never question you about the basics. They never tell you, "What is the sound of his voice?" What games does he prefer? Does he collect butterflies? They ask, "How old is he?" How many brothers? How much does he weigh? How much does his father earn? Then they only think they know him. If you say to the grown-ups: "I saw a beautiful pink brick house, with geraniums on the windows and doves on the roof ..." they cannot imagine this house. We must say to them: "I have seen a house of one hundred thousand francs. Then they cried: "How pretty it is! "

So, if you say to them: "The proof that the little prince existed is that he was delightful, that he laughed, and that he wanted a sheep. When you want a sheep, it is proof that you exist, "they will shrug their shoulders and treat you as a child! But if you tell them, "The planet where it came from is asteroid B 612" then they will be convinced, and they will leave you alone with their questions. They're like that. We must not blame them. Children should be very lenient towards adults.

But, of course, we who understand life, we make fun of the numbers! I would have liked to start this story like fairy tales. I would have liked to say:

"Once upon a time there was a little prince who lived on a planet hardly larger than himself, and who needed a friend ..." For those who understand life, it would have seemed much truer.

Because I do not like to read my book lightly. I feel so sorry to recount these memories. It's six years since my friend went away with his sheep. If I try to describe it here, it is so as not to forget it. It's sad to forget a friend. Not everyone has had a friend. And I can become like the grown-ups who are interested only in numbers. So that's why I bought a box of colors and pencils. It's hard to go back to drawing, at my age, when no other attempt has ever been made than that of a closed boa and that of an open boa at the age of six! I will try, of course, to make portraits as resembling as possible. But I'm not quite

Sure, I'm going to succeed. One drawing goes, and the other does not look any more. I make some errors, also on the size. Here the little prince is too big. There he is too small. I also hesitate about the color of his costume. Then I fumbled like this and that, as best I could. At last, I shall be mistaken about certain more important details. But that will have to be forgiven. My friend never gave an explanation. He thought I might be like him. But I, unfortunately, I do not know how to see the sheep through the crates. I may be a bit like grown-ups. I must have got older.

V

Every day I learned something on the planet, on departure, on the journey. It came very gently at the chance of reflections. Thus, on the third day, I knew the drama of the baobabs.

This time again it was thanks to the sheep, for suddenly the little prince interrogated me, as if caught in a serious doubt:

"It is true, is it not, that sheep eat the shrubs?"

Yes. That is true. "Ah! I am happy! "

I did not understand why it was so important that the sheep ate the shrubs. But the little prince added:

"So, they also eat the baobabs?" "

I remarked to the little prince that the baobab trees are not shrubs, but trees as large as churches, and that even if they carried with them a whole herd of elephants, this flock would not be able to overcome a single baobab.

The idea of the herd of elephants made the little prince laugh:

"We should put them on top of each other ..."

But he remarked wisely:

"The baobabs, before growing, it starts off being small.

That's right! But why do you want your sheep to eat the little baobabs? "

He replied, "Well! Come on! "As it was obvious. And it took me a great effort of intelligence to understand to myself this problem.

And indeed, on the planet of the little prince, there was, as on all the planets, good grasses, and weeds. Therefore, good seeds of good weeds and bad seeds of weeds. But the seeds are invisible. They sleep in the secret of the earth until it takes fancy for one of them to wake up. Then she stretched herself, and at first shoved timidly toward the sun a ravishing little harmless little twig. If it is a twig of radish or rose bush, you can let it grow as it wants. But if it is a bad plant, it is necessary to tear the plant immediately, as soon as it is known to recognize it. Now there were terrible seeds on the planet of the little prince ... these were the seeds of baobabs. The soil of the planet was infested. Now a baobab, if one takes it too late, one can never get rid of it anymore. It encumbers the whole planet. He is performing her with his roots. And if the planet is too small, and if the baobabs are too numerous, they make it burst.

"It's a matter of discipline," the little prince later told me. When you have finished your morning toilet, you have to do the toilet of the planet carefully. It is necessary to regularly bite the baobabs as soon as they are distinguished from the roses to which they resemble very much when they are very young. It's a very boring job, but very easy. "

And one day he advised me to apply myself to a beautiful drawing, in order to bring it into the heads of the children of my house. "If they travel one day," he said to me, "that could serve them. It is sometimes inconvenient to postpone his work. But if it is a question of the baobabs, it is always a catastrophe. I knew a planet, inhabited by a lazy. He had neglected three shrubs ... "

And, on the instructions of the little prince, I drew this planet. I do not like to take the tone of a moralist. But the danger of the baobabs is so little known, and the risks run by the one wandering in an asteroid are so considerable, that for once I am an exception to my reserve. I said, "Children! Pay attention to the baobabs! It was to warn my friends of the

danger that they had been for a long time, like myself, without knowing it, that I had worked so much on this drawing. The lesson I gave was worth it. You may wonder: Why are there no other drawings in this book as grandiose as the drawing of the baobabs? The answer is very simple: I tried but I could not succeed. When I drew the baobabs, I was animated by the feeling of urgency.

VI

Ah! Little prince, I have understood, little by little, your little melancholy life. You had only for a long distraction the sweetness of the sunsets. I learned this new detail, on the fourth day in the morning, when you said to me:

"I like the sunsets. Let's see a sunset ...

But you have to wait...

Wait for what?

Wait until the sun goes down. "

You looked very surprised at first, and then you laughed at yourself. And you said to me:

" I always feel at home! "

Indeed. When it is noon in the United States, the sun, as everyone knows, lies on France. It would be enough to be able to go to France in one minute to watch the sunset. Unfortunately, France is far too far away. But, on your little planet, it was enough for you to pull your chair a few steps. And you were watching twilight whenever you wished …

"One day I saw the sun go down forty-four times! "

And a little later you added:

"You know … when you're so sad you like the sunsets …" "So, the day of the forty-four times you were so sad?" "But the little prince did not answer.

VII

The fifth day, always thanks to the sheep, this secret of the life of the little prince was revealed to me. He asked me brusquely, without preamble, as the fruit of a problem long meditated in silence:

"A sheep, if he eats the shrubs, he also eats the flowers?" "A sheep eats whatever he meets." "Even flowers that have thorns?"

Yes. Even flowers that have thorns. "Then the thorns, what are they for?" "

I did not know. I was then very busy trying to unscrew a too tight bolt from my engine. I was very worried because my breakdown was beginning to appear very serious, and the drinking water that was exhausted made me fear the worst.

"Thorns, what are they used for?" "

The little prince never renounced a question once

he had asked it. I was irritated by my bolt, and I answered no matter what:

"Thorns are useless, it's pure wickedness on the part of flowers!

Oh! "

But after a pause he threw me, with a sort of rancor:

" I do not believe you! Flowers are weak. They are naive. They reassure themselves as best they can. They think they are terrible with their thorns … "

I made no reply. At that moment I said to myself: "If this bolt still resists, I'll blow it up with a hammer. The little prince again disturbed my reflections:

"And you think that flowers …"

But no! But no! I do not believe anything! I answered anything. I am busy with serious things! "

He looked at me stunned.

"Serious things! "

He saw me, with my hammer in my hand, and my fingers black with shimmering, bending over an object which seemed very ugly to him.

"You talk like grown-ups!" "

It made me a little ashamed. But, pitiless, he added:

"You confuse everything ... you mix everything! "

He was really very irritated. He shook the gilded hair in the wind:

"I know a planet where there is a crimson gentleman. He never breathed a flower. He never looked at a star. He never loved anyone. He has never done anything other than additions. And all day he repeats like you: "I am a serious man! I am a serious man!" And it makes him swell with pride. But it's not a man, it's a mushroom!

A what?

Λ fungus! "

The little prince was now pale with anger.

"Millions of years ago flowers make thorns. Millions of years ago the sheep still eat the flowers. And it is not serious to try to understand why they are doing so much trouble to make thorns that are never used for anything? It's not important the war of sheep and flowers? This is not serious and more important than the additions of a big red gentleman? And if I know a flower unique in the world, which exists nowhere, except in my planet, and a little sheep can annihilate at once, like that, one morning, without realizing What he does is not important! “

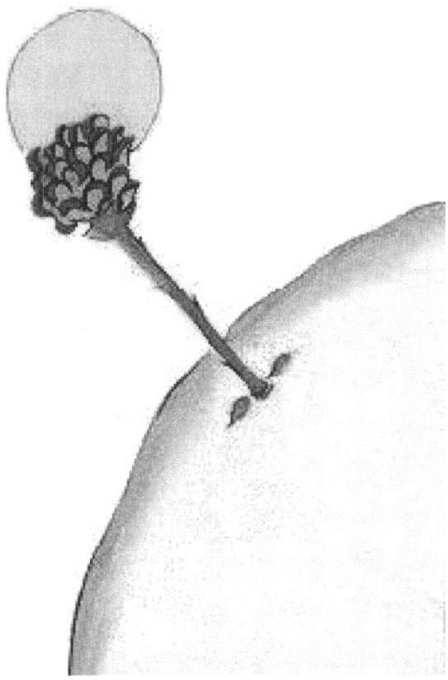

He blushed, then resumed:

“If someone loves a flower that only exists in one million and millions of stars, that’s enough for him to be happy when he looks at them. He said to himself: “My flower is there somewhere …” But if the sheep eats the flower, it is for him as if, suddenly, all the stars were extinguished! And that’s not important! “

He could say nothing more. He suddenly burst into tears. Night had fallen. I had let go of my tools. I made fun of my hammer, my bolt, my thirst, and my death. There was on a star, a planet, mine, the Earth, a little prince to console! I took him in my arms. I rocked him. I said to him: "The flower you love is not in danger … I will draw a muzzle to your sheep

… I will draw an armor for your flower … I …" I did not know what to say. I felt very awkward. I did not know how to reach it, where to join it … It is so mysterious, the land of tears!

VIII

I soon learned more about this flower. There had always been very simple flowers on the planet of the little prince, adorned with a single row of petals, and which held no room, and which did not disturb anyone. They appeared one morning in the grass, and then they were extinguished in the evening. But that one had germinated one day, of a seed brought from somewhere, and the little prince had watched very closely that twig that did not resemble the other twigs. It could be a new kind of baobab. But the shrub soon ceased to grow and began to prepare a flower. The little prince, who was watching the installation of an enormous button, felt that a miraculous apparition would emerge, but the flower did not finish preparing to be beautiful, sheltered from his green room. She carefully chose her colors. She dressed slowly she adjusted her petals one by one. She did not want to get out of it all like the poppies. She wanted to appear only in the full radiance of her beauty. Hey! Yes. She was very coquette! His mysterious dress had lasted days and days. And then one morning, just at sunrise, she had shown herself.

And she, who had worked so precisely, said in yawning:

"Ah! I'm just waking up ... I beg your pardon ... I'm still disheveled ... "

The little prince, then, could not contain his admiration:

" How beautiful you are!

"Is not that right," the flower replied softly. And I was born at the same time as the sun ...

"The little prince guessed that she was not too modest, but she was so moving!"It's time, I think, for breakfast," she would soon add, "would you have the kindness to think of me?"

And the little prince, quite confused, having sought a watering-can of fresh water, had served the flower.

So had she quickly tormented him by his somewhat shady vanity. One day, for example, speaking of her four thorns, she had said to the little prince:

"They can come, the tigers, with their claws!

“There are no tigers on my planet,” objected the little prince, “and then the tigers do not eat grass.”

I am not a grass, had gently replied to the flower.

Excuse me…

“I have no fear of tigers, but I hate currents of air.” You would not have a screen?

"Horror of drafts … it is not luck, for a plant, had noticed the little prince. This flower is very complicated … »

"In the evening you will put me under a globe. It's very cold at home. It's badly installed. Where I come from… "

But she had interrupted herself. It had come in the form of a seed. She had not known anything about other worlds. Humiliated at having allowed herself to be surprised at preparing such a naive lie, she coughed two or three times to put the little prince into his wrong:

"This screen?" …

I was going to get him, but you were talking to me! " Then she had forced her cough to inflict remorse.

Thus, the little prince, notwithstanding the goodwill of his love, soon doubted her. He had taken unimportant words seriously and had become very unhappy.

"I should not have listened to him," he confided to me one day, "you must never listen to flowers. You have to look at them and breathe them. Mine embalmed my planet, but I could not rejoice. This story of claws, which had so annoyed me, should have tempted me ... "

He again confided to me:

"I did not understand anything! I should have judged her on the acts and not the words. She embarrassed me and enlightened me. I should never have fled! I should have guessed his tenderness behind his poor tricks. The flowers are so contradictory! But I was too young to know how to love him. "

IX

Je crois qu'il profita, pour son évasion, d'une migration d'oiseaux sauvages.

I believe that he took advantage of a migration of wild birds for his escape. On the morning of the departure, he put his planet in order. He carefully roamed his active volcanoes. He had two active volcanoes. And it was very convenient to warm up the morning breakfast. He also possessed an extinct volcano. But, as he said, "You never know!" He therefore also roamed the extinct volcano. If they are well swept, volcanoes burn gently and regularly, without eruptions. Volcanic eruptions are like chimney fires. Obviously on our land we are much too small to swallow our volcanoes. That's why they're causing us a lot of trouble.

The little prince also snatched, with a little melancholy, the last shoots of baobabs. He thought he would never have to come back. But all these familiar labors appeared to him, that morning, extremely sweet. And when he watered the flower for the last time, and prepared to shelter it under his globe, he discovered the desire to weep.

"Farewell," he said to the flower.

But she did not answer.

"Farewell," he repeated.

The flower coughed. But it was not because of his cold.

"I was a fool," she said at last. I beg your pardon. Strive to be happy. "

He was surprised by the absence of reproaches. He remained there, disconcerted, the globe in the air. He did not understand this quiet sweetness.

"Yes, I love you," said the flower. You did not know, by my fault. It has no importance. But you were as stupid as I was. Task to be happy … Leave this globe quiet. I do not want it anymore.

But the wind …

I'm not so cold as that … The cool air of the night will do me good. I'm a flower.

But the beasts …

"I must bear two or three caterpillars if I want to know the butterflies." It seems that it is so beautiful. Otherwise, who will visit me? You will be far away. As for the big beasts, I fear nothing. I have my claws. "

And she naively showed her four thorns. Then she added:

"Do not drag like that, it's annoying. You decided to leave. Go away. " For, she did not want him to see her crying. It was such a proud flower.....

X

He was in the region of the asteroids 325, 326, 327, 328, 329 and 330. He therefore began by visiting them to search for an occupation and to learn.

The first was inhabited by a king. The king sat, dressed in purple and ermine, on a very simple and yet majestic throne.

"Ah! Here is a subject! Cried the king when he

perceived the little prince.

And the little prince asked himself:

"How can he recognize me since he has never seen me before?" "

He did not know that for kings, the world is very simplified. All men are subjects.

"Come closer, I'll see you better," said the king, who was very proud to be king at last.

The little prince sought eyes to sit down, but the planet was cluttered with the magnificent ermine mantle. So, he stood and as he was tired, he yawned.

"It is contrary to the etiquette of yawning in the presence of a king," said the monarch. I forbid it.

"I cannot help myself," replied the little prince, quite confused. I did a long trip, and I did not sleep …

"Then," said the king, "I command you to yawn." I have not seen anyone yawning for years. Yawns are curiosities for me. Come on! Still yawns. It's an order.

"That intimidates me … I cannot …" said the little prince, blushing.

Um! Hum! Replied the king. Then I ... I order you to yawn and sometimes to ... "He stammered a little and seemed vexed.

For the King was essentially concerned that his authority should be respected. He did not tolerate disobedience. He was an absolute monarch. But as he was very good, he gave reasonable orders.

"If I commanded," said he, "if I ordered a general to change into a sea-bird and if the general did not obey, it would not be the general's fault." It would be my fault. "

" May I sit? Inquired the little prince, timidly.

"I order you to sit down," replied the king, who brought back majestically a piece of his ermine cloak.

But the little prince was astonished. The planet was tiny. On what could the king reign?

"Sire," said he, "I beg your pardon to ask you questions."

"I order you to question me," said the King.

"Sire, on what do you reign?"

"Above all," replied the king, with great simplicity.

Mostly? "

The king, with a discreet gesture, pointed to his planet, the other planets, and the stars.

"About all that?" Said the little prince.

"On all that," replied the king.

For not only was he an absolute monarch but he was a universal monarch.

"And the stars obey you?"

"Of course," said the king. They obey at once. I do not tolerate indiscipline. "

Such a power marveled the little prince. If he had relaxed it himself, he might have been present, not at forty-four, but at seventy-two, or even a hundred, or even two hundred sunsets in the same day, To pull his chair! And as he felt a little sad because of the memory of his little abandoned planet, he boldly solicited a favor from the king:

"I would like to see a sunset … Do me a favor … Order the sun to lie down …

"If I ordered a general to fly from one flower to another like a butterfly, or write a tragedy, or change into a seabird and if the general did not execute The order received, which of him or of me would be in his wrong?

"It would be you," said the little prince firmly.

Exact. We must demand of each one what each one can give, "replied the king. Authority rests first on reason. If thou commandest thy people to go throw themselves into the sea, they shall make a revolution. I have the right to demand obedience because my orders are reasonable.

"Then my sunset?" Reminded the little prince, who never forgot a question once he had asked it.

Your sunset, you will have it. I will demand it. But I shall wait, in my science of the government, for the conditions to be favorable.

"When will it be?" Inquired the little prince.

Hem! Hem! Replied the king, who at first consulted a large calendar, "hem! Hem! It will be, towards-towards-it will be this evening towards seven forty! And you will see how well I am obeyed. "

The little prince yawned. He regretted his failed sunset. And then he was already bored a little:

"I have nothing more to do here," he said to the king. I'll go again!

"Do not go," replied the king, who was so proud of

having a subject. Do not go, I make you a minister!

Minister of what?

Of ... of Justice!

"But there is no one to judge!"

"We do not know," said the king. I have not yet gone round my kingdom. I am very old, I have no place for a coach, and it tires me to walk.

Oh! But I have already seen, "said the little prince, who bent down to glance at the other side of the planet. There's no one there either

"You will judge yourself, then," replied the king. This is the most difficult. It is much more difficult to judge oneself than to judge others. If you manage to judge yourself well, it is because you are a true wise man.

"I," said the little prince, "can judge myself anywhere." I do not need to live here.

Hem! Hem! Said the king, "I believe that on my planet there is somewhere an old rat. I hear it at night. You can judge that old rat. You will condemn him to death from time to time. So, his life will depend on your righteousness. But you will pardon it every time to save it. There is only one.

"I," replied the little prince, "do not like to condemn to death, and I believe I am going."

"No," said the king.

But the little prince, having finished his preparations, would not trouble the old monarch:

"If your majesty wished to be obeyed punctually," she might give me a reasonable order. She could order me, for example, to leave before one minute. It seems to me that the conditions are favorable … "

The king having replied nothing, the little prince hesitated at first, then, with a sigh, took the departure.

"I make you my ambassador," then hastened to cry the king.

He had an air of authority.

Great people are very strange, the little prince said to himself, during his journey.,

XI

The second planet was inhabited by a conceited man:

"Ah! Ah! Here is the visit of an admirer! Exclaimed the vanity from a distance as soon as he saw the little prince.

For, for the conceited, other men are admirers.

“Good morning,” said the little prince. You have a funny hat.

“It is to salute,” replied the conceited. It is to greet when I am acclaimed. Unfortunately, it never passes anybody here.

Ah, yes? Said the little prince, who did not understand.

“Strike your hands one against the other,” advised the conceited man.

The little prince struck his hands against each other. The conceited man modestly saluted his hat.

“This is more amusing than the visit to the king,” said the little prince to himself. And he

began again to strike his hands one against the other. The conceited man began to salute, raising his hat.

After five minutes of exercise the little prince got tired of the monotony of the game:

“And so that the hat falls,” he asked, “what is to be done? “

But the vein did not hear it. Vainites never hear anything but praise.

"Do you really admire me a lot? He asked the little prince.

What does it mean to admire?

To admire means to recognize that I am the most beautiful, the best dressed, the richest and the most intelligent man on the planet.

But you're alone on your planet!

Make me this pleasure. Admire me anyway!

"I admire you," said the little prince, shrugging his shoulders a little, "but how can that interest you?"

And the little prince departed.

"The grown-ups are decidedly bizarre," he told himself simply during his journey.

XII

The next planet was inhabited by a drinker. This visit was very short, but she plunged the little prince into a great melancholy:

"What are you doing here? He said to the drinker, whom he found installed in silence before a collection of empty bottles and a collection of full bottles.

"I drink," replied the drinker, with a lugubrious air.

"Why do you drink?" Asked the little prince.

"To forget," replied the drinker.

To forget what? Inquired the little prince, who already pitied him.

"To forget that I am ashamed," confessed the drinker, lowering his head.

"Shame on what? Inquired the little prince who wished to succor him.

"Shame on you to drink! Finished the drinker, who locked himself up in silence.

And the little prince left, puzzled.

"Big people are definitely very bizarre," he told himself during the trip.,

XIII

The fourth planet was that of the businessman. This man was so busy that he did not even raise his head at the arrival of the little prince.

"Good morning," said the latter. Your cigarette is extinguished.

Three and two are five. Five and seven twelve. Twelve and three. Hello. Fifteen and ninety-two. Twenty-two and six-eight. No time to turn it back on. Twenty-six and five thirty-one. Phew! So, it's five hundred one million six hundred twenty-two thousand seven hundred and thirty-one.

"Five hundred million of what?"

Hey? You're still here? Five hundred a million ... I do not know ... I have so much work! I am serious, I do not amuse myself with nonsense! Two and five ...

- Five hundred million of what? "Repeated the little prince, who, in his life, had never renounced a question once he had asked it.

The businessman raised his head:

"For the past fifty-four years I have lived on this planet, I have only been disturbed three times. The first time it was twenty-two years ago, by a cock-chart that had fallen, God knows where. He spread a terrible noise, and I made four errors in an addition. The second time, eleven years ago, was a crisis of rheumatism. I lack exercise. I do not have time to stroll. I'm serious. The third time ... here it is! So, I said five hundred million ...

Millions of what? "

The businessman understood that there was no hope of peace:

"Millions of these little things that one sees sometimes in the sky.

Flies?

But no, little things that shine.

Bees?

But no. Little golden things that make the idlers laugh. But I am serious! I do not have time to daydream.

"Ah! stars?

That's right. Stars.

"And what do you do with five hundred million stars?"

Five hundred and one million six hundred and twenty-two thousand seven hundred and thirty-one. I am serious, I am precise.

"And what do you do with these stars?"

What do I do with it?

Yes.

Nothing. I own them.

You got the stars?

Yes.

"But I've already seen a king who"

Kings do not possess. They "reign" over. It is very different. "And what is the use of possessing the stars?"It's good for me to be rich.

"And what does it cost you to be rich?"

To buy other stars if someone finds them. "

"That one," said the little prince to himself, "he reasoned a little like my drunkard. "

However, he asked further questions:

"How can one possess the stars?"

Who are they? Riposta, grumpy, businessman.

I do not know. To no one.

"Then they belong to me, for I thought of it first."

That's enough?

Of course. When you find a diamond that belongs to no one, it is yours. When you find an island that belongs to no one, it is yours. When you have an idea first, you patent it, it is yours. And I possess the stars since no one before me thought of possessing them.

"That is true," said the little prince. And what do you do with it?

I deal with them. I count them and recount them, says the businessman. It's difficult. But I'm a serious man! "

The little prince was not satisfied yet.

"If I have a scarf, I can put it around my neck and take it away." I, if I possess a flower, can pluck my flower, and carry it away. But you cannot pick the stars!

"No, but I can put them in a bank."

What does it mean?

"That means I write on a little paper the number of my stars. And then I lock this paper in a drawer.

And that's all?

That's enough! "

"It's amusing," thought the little prince. It's pretty poetic. But it is not very serious. "

The little prince had very different ideas about the serious things of the ideas of the grown-up.

"I," he said again, "have a flower that I water every

day. I have three volcanoes that I shake every week. For I also sweep away the extinct one. We never know. It is useful to my volcanoes, and it is useful to my flower, that I possess them. But you are not useful to the stars … "

The businessman opened his mouth but found no answer and the little prince left.

"The grown-ups are definitely quite extraordinary," he said simply to himself during the journey.,

XIV

The fifth planet was very curious. It was the smallest of them all. There was just enough room to house a lamppost and a streetlamp lighter. The little prince could not explain how a streetlamp and a lamp-lighter could be used, somewhere in the sky, on a planet without a house or a population. However, he said to himself:

"Maybe this man is absurd. However, it is less absurd than the king, the vein, the businessman and the drinker. At least his work makes sense. When he lights his lamppost, it is as if he were creating another star, or a flower. When he turns off his lamppost, it puts the flower or the star to sleep. It is a very pretty occupation. This is really useful since it is beautiful. "

When he approached the planet, he greeted the lighter respectfully:

" Hello. Why did you just turn off your streetlamp? "That is the order," replied the lighter. Hello. "What is the deposit?""It is to extinguish my lamppost." Good evening. "And he rekindled it."But why have you just turned it on?"

"That is the order," replied the lighter.

"I do not understand," said the little prince.

"There is nothing to understand," said the lighter. The setpoint is the setpoint. Hello."

And he put out his streetlamp.

Then he wiped his forehead with a red-checked handkerchief.

"I am doing a terrible trade there. It was reasonable in the past. I switched off in the morning and switched on at night. I had the rest of the day to rest, and the rest of the night to sleep ..."

"And since that time the order has changed?"

"The order has not changed," said the lighter. That is the tragedy! The planet from year to year has turned faster and faster, and the deposit has not changed!

So? Said the little prince.

"So now that she is doing one turn a minute, I have no more rest." I turn on and off once a minute!

Now that's funny! The days at your house last a minute!

"It's not funny at all," said the lighter. It's been a month since we've been talking together.

A month?

Yes. Thirty minutes. Thirty days! Good evening. "And he reignited his lamppost.

The little prince looked at him and he loved this lighter who was so faithful to the instructions. He remembered the sunsets that he himself once went looking for, drawing his chair. He wanted to help his friend:

"You know … I know a way to rest when you want …" "I always want," said the lighter. For one can be both faithful and lazy. The little prince continued:

"Your planet is so small that you go around it in three strides. You only have to walk slowly to stay in the sun. When you want to rest you will walk … and the day will last as long as you want.

"It does not help me much," said the lighter. What I like about life is sleeping.

"It's not lucky," said the little prince.

"No luck," said the lighter. Hello. "

And he put out his streetlamp.

"That one," said the little prince, "as he pursued his journey further, he would be despised by all the others, by the king, by the vein, by the drinker, by the businessman." However,

it is the only one that does not seem ridiculous to me. It is, perhaps, because he cares about nothing but himself. "

He sighed with regret and said to himself again:

“This is the only one I could have made my friend. But his planet is really too small. There is no room for two … »

What the little prince did not dare to admit was that he regretted this blessed planet because, above all, of the thousand four hundred and forty sunsets in twenty-four hours!,

XV

The sixth planet was a planet ten times larger. It was inhabited by an old gentleman who wrote enormous books.

“Here! Here is an explorer! Cried he, when he perceived the little prince.

The little prince sat down on the table and breathed a little. He already had traveled so much!

”Where do you come from? Said the old gentleman.

-What is this big book? Said the little prince. What are you doing here? "I am a geographer," said the old gentleman. "What is a geographer?"

"He is a scientist who knows where the seas, rivers, cities, mountains, and deserts are.

"That is very interesting," said the little prince. It's finally a real job! And he cast a glance around him on the geographer's planet. He had never seen a planet so majestic.

"It is very beautiful, your planet. Are there oceans?

"I cannot know," said the geographer.

"Ah! (The little prince was disappointed.) And mountains?

"I cannot know," said the geographer.

"And cities and rivers and deserts?"

"I cannot know it either," said the geographer.

"But you are a geographer!

"That's right," said the geographer, "but I am not an explorer. I absolutely lack explorers. It is not the geographer who will count cities, rivers, mountains, seas, oceans, and deserts. The geographer is too important to stroll. He does not leave his office.

But he receives the explorers there. He interrogates them and takes note of their memories. And if the memories of one of them seem interesting to him, the geographer makes investigate the morality of the explorer.

Why this?

"Because an explorer who lies would cause catastrophes in the books of geography." And also, an explorer who would drink too much.

Why this? Said the little prince.

"Because drunks see double."Then the geographer would note two mountains, where there is only one.

"I know somebody," said the little prince, who would be a bad explorer.

It's possible. So, when the morality of the explorer seems good, an inquiry is made into his discovery.

We will, see?

No. It's too complicated. But the explorer is required to provide evidence. If, for example, the discovery of a large mountain is required, it is required to bring large stones.

"The geographer was suddenly moved.

“But you come from a distance! You’re an explorer! You’re going to describe your planet! “

And the geographer, having opened his register, cut his pencil. We first note in pencil the narratives of the explorers. It is expected, to note in ink, that the explorer has provided evidence.

” So? Inquired the geographer.

Oh! At home, “said the little prince,” it’s not very interesting, it’s very small. I have three volcanoes. Two active volcanoes, and an extinct volcano. But we never know.

“You never know,” said the geographer.

I also have a flower.

“We do not notice flowers,” said the geographer.

Why this! This is the nicest! “Because flowers are ephemeral.”

What does ‘ephemeral’ mean?

“Geographies,” said the geographer, “are the most serious books in all books. They never go out of style. It is very rare that a mountain changes its place. It is very rare that an ocean empties its water. We write eternal things.

"But the extinct volcanoes can wake up," interrupted the little prince. What does "ephemeral" mean?

"Whether volcanoes are extinguished or awakened is the same for us," said the geographer. What matters to us is the mountain. It does not change.

"But what does" ephemeral "mean? Repeated the little prince, who had never given up a question in his life once he had asked it.

It means "who is threatened with the near disappearance".

My flower is threatened with disappearance soon.

Of course.

"My flower is ephemeral," thought the little prince, "and she has only four thorns to defend herself against the world! And I left her alone with me! "

This was his first movement of regret. But he resumed his courage:

"What do you advise me to visit?" He asked.

"Planet Earth," replied the geographer. She has a good reputation ... "

And the little prince went away, thinking of his flower.

XVI

The seventh planet was therefore the Earth.

The Earth is not a planet of any kind! There are a hundred and eleven kings (not forgetting, of course, the Negro kings), seven thousand geographers, nine hundred thousand businessmen, seven and a half million drunkards, three hundred and eleven million vain, About two billion large people.

To give you an idea of the dimensions of the Earth, I will tell you that before the invention of electricity there was to be maintained on all six continents a genuine army of four hundred and sixty-two thousand five hundred and eleven lighters Of streetlamps.

Seen from a little distance it made a splendid effect. The movements of this army were regulated like those of an operatic ballet. First came the turn of streetlamp lighters from New Zealand and Australia. Then, having lit their lanterns, they went to sleep.

Then the

dancers of the lamps of China and Siberia entered the dance. Then they also slipped backstage. Then came the turn of the lighters of streetlamps of Russia and the Indies. Then those of Africa and Europe. Then those of South America. Then those of North America. And they never erred in their order of entry. It was great.

Only the lighter of the single streetlamp of the North Pole, and his colleague of the only streetlamp of the South Pole, led lives of idleness and nonchalance: they worked twice a year.

XVII

When one wants to make the mind, it happens that one lying a little. I was not very honest in telling you about street light lighter. I risk giving a false idca of our planet to those who do not know it. Men occupy very little space on earth. If the two billion inhabitants who inhabit the land were standing up and a little tight, as if for a meeting, they would easily lodge in a public square twenty miles long and twenty miles wide. We could put humanity on the smallest little island in the Pacific.

Great people, of course, will not believe you. They imagine they hold a lot of space. They see themselves important as baobabs. You will advise them to do the calculation. They love the numbers: it will please them. But do not waste your time on this pensum. It's useless. You trust me.

The little prince, once on land, was therefore much surprised to see no one. He was already afraid of being mistaken about the planet when a ring of moonlight stirred in the sand.

"Good night," said the little prince, at all hazards.

"Good night," said the serpent.

-On what planet have I fallen? Asked the little prince. "On the Earth, in Africa," replied the serpent.

"Ah! … So, there is nobody on Earth?

"Here is the desert." There is no one in the deserts. The Earth is great, "says the serpent. The little prince sat down on a stone and raised his eyes to the sky:

"I wonder," he said, "if the stars are illuminated so that everyone can one day find his own. Look at my planet. She's just above us ... But how far she is!

"She is beautiful," said the serpent. What are you doing here?

"I have difficulties with a flower," said the little prince.

"Ah! The serpent said.

And they were silent.

" Where are the men? Resumed the little prince. We're a little alone in the desert ... "One is also alone among men," said the serpent. The little prince looked at him for a long time:

"You are a funny beast," he said at last, thin as a

finger.

"But I am more powerful than the finger of a king," said the serpent.

The little prince smiled:

"You're not very powerful ... you do not even have paws ... you cannot even travel ... "I can carry you farther than a ship," said the serpent.He wrapped himself around the ankle of the little prince, like a gold bracelet:

"The one I touch, I return to the earth from which he came out," he said again. But you are pure, and you come from a star ... "

The little prince answered nothing.

"You pity me you so weak, on this Granite Earth. I can help you someday if you regret too much your planet. I can...

Oh! I understood very well, "said the little prince," but why do you always speak in riddles?

"I will resolve them all," said the serpent.And they fell silent.

XVIII

The little prince crossed the desert and met only a flower. A flower with three petals, a flower of nothing at all …

"Good morning," said the little prince.

"Good morning," said the flower.

Where are the men? The little prince asked politely. The flower, one day, had seen a caravan pass:"

Men? There are, I believe, six or seven of them. I saw them years ago. But you never know where to find them. The wind sends them rambling. They lack roots, they are very embarrassed.

"Good-bye," said the little prince.

"Adieu," said the flower.

XIX

The little prince ascended a high mountain. The only mountains he had ever known were the three volcanoes that came to his knee. And he used the cxtinct volcano as a stool. "From a mountain high like this," he said to himself, "I shall suddenly see the whole planet and all the men." But he perceived nothing but sharp needles of rock.

"Good morning," he said at random.

Hello … Hello … Hello … replied to the echo.

Who are you? Said the little prince.

"Who are you? Who are you? Who are you?" Replied the echo.

"Be my friends, I am alone," he said.

"I am alone … I am alone … I am alone …" replied the echo.

"What a strange planet! He thought then. It is quite dry, and all pointed and salty. And men lack imagination. They repeat what they are told … At home I had a flower: it always spoke first … "

XX

But it happened that the little prince, having for a long time walked through the sands, the rocks, and the snows, at length discovered a road. And the roads all go to men.

"Good morning," he said.

It was a garden full of roses.

"Good morning," said the roses.

The little prince looked at them. They all looked like her flower.

"Who are you? He asked, stunned. "We are roses," said the roses. "Ah! Said the little prince.

And he felt very unhappy. Her flower had told him that she was the only one of her kind in the universe. And there were five thousand, all alike, in one garden!

"She would be very upset," he said to herself, "if she saw that-she would cough so much and pretend to die to escape ridicule." And I would be obliged to pretend to treat her, for otherwise, to humiliate me too, she would really let herself die … "

Then he said to himself again: "I thought myself rich with a single flower, and I possess only an ordinary rose. That and my three volcanoes which reach me at the knee, and one of which, perhaps, is extinct forever, does not make me a great prince … "And, lying in the grass, he will cry.

XXI

And then the Fox appeared:

"Good morning," said the fox.

"Good morning," replied the little prince, politely, who turned, but saw nothing. "I am here," said the voice, "under the apple-tree."

Who are you? Said the little prince. You're quite pretty... "I am a fox," said the fox.

"Come play with me," suggested the little prince.

I'm so sad… "I cannot play with you," said the fox. I am not domesticated. "Ah! Pardon, "said the little prince.

But after reflection, he added: " What does "tame" mean " ?

"You're not from here," said the fox, "what are you looking for?"

"I am looking for men," said the little prince. What does "tame" mean"?

"Men," said the fox, "they have rifles, and they hunt." It is very embarrassing! They also breed chickens. That is their only interest. Are you looking for chickens?

"No," said the little prince. I am looking for some friends. What does "tame" mean? "It's too forgotten," said the fox. It means "Create links …" Create links?"Of course," said the fox. You are but a little boy to me, like a hundred thousand little boys. And I do not need you. And you do not need me either. I am only a fox to you like a hundred thousand foxes. But if you take me, we will need one another. You will be unique in the world for me. I will be for you unique in the world …

"I begin to understand," said the little prince. There is a flower … I think she tamed me … "It is possible," said the fox. We see all sorts of things on Earth …

Oh! It is not on Earth, "said the little prince. The fox seemed very intrigued:

"On another planet"?

Yes.

"There are hunters on this planet?"

No.

That's interesting! And hens?

No.

"Nothing is perfect," the fox sighed.

But the fox returned to his idea:

“My life is monotonous. I chase chickens, men chase me. All the chickens resemble each-other, and all men are alike. So, I’m a little bored. But if you take me, my life will be as sunny. I will experience a footstep that will be different from all the others. The other steps make me go underground. Yours will call me out of the burrow, like a music. And look! You see, over there, the fields of wheat? I do not eat bread. Wheat for me is useless. The wheat fields do not remind me of anything. And that’s sad! But you have golden hair. Then it will be wonderful when you have tamed me! The wheat, which is gilded, will make me remember you. And I will love the sound of the wind in wheat … “

The fox fell silent and looked at the little prince for a long time:

“Please … tame me!” “He said.

“I will,” replied the little prince, “but I have not much time.” I have friends to discover and a lot to know.

“We only know the things we tame,” said the fox. Men no longer have the time to know anything. They buy ready-made things from merchants. But as there are no merchants of friends, men no longer have friends. If you want a friend, tame me!

What should be done? Said the little prince.

"You must be very patient," replied the fox. You will sit first a little far from me, like that, in the grass. I will look at you from the corner of your eye and you will not say anything. Language is a source of misunderstanding. But every day you can sit a little closer … "

The next day the little prince returned.

"It would have been better to return at the same hour," said the fox. If you come, for example, at four o'clock in the afternoon, at three o'clock I shall begin to be happy. The more time will come, the happier

I will feel. At four o'clock I shall be agitated and worried; I shall discover the price of happiness! But if you come anytime, I will never know what time to dress my heart … it takes rites.

"What is a rite?" Said the little prince.

"It's too much forgotten," said the fox. This is what makes one day different from other days, one-hour, other hours. There is a rite, for example, among my hunters. They dance on Thursday with the girls of the village. Then Thursday is a wonderful day! I'll walk up the vineyard. If the hunters danced at any time, the days would all be alike, and I would have no holiday. "

So, the little prince tamed the fox. And when the hour of departure was near:

"Ah! Said the fox, "I will weep."

"It is your fault," said the little prince, "I did not wish you any harm, but you wanted me to tame you."

"Of course," said the fox.

"But you're going to cry!" Said the little prince.

"Of course," said the fox.

"Then you gain nothing!"

"I win," said the fox, "because of the color of the corn."

Then he added:

"Go and see the roses again. You will understand that yours is unique in the world. You will return to say good-bye to me, and I will make you a present of a secret. "

The little prince went to see the roses again.

"You are not at all like my rose, you are nothing yet," he said. No one has tamed you and you have not tamed anyone. You're like was my fox. It was only a fox like a hundred thousand others. But I made him my friend, and he is now unique in the world. "

And the roses were very embarrassed.

"You are beautiful, but you are empty," he said again. You cannot die for you. Of course, my rose, an ordinary passer-by would think that she resembles you. But it alone is more important than you all, since it is she that I watered. Since it was, she whom I placed under the globe, since it was, she whom I sheltered by the screen. Since it is she whose caterpillars I have killed (except the two or three for butterflies). Since it is she whom I have listened to, complaining, or boasting, or even sometimes silent. Since it is my rose. "

And he returned to the fox:

"Adieu," he said.

"Good-bye," said the fox. Here is my secret. It is very simple: one sees only with the heart. What is essential is invisible to the eye.

"The essential thing is invisible to the eyes," repeated the little prince, in order to remember.

It's the time you lost for your rose that makes your rose so important.

"It's the time I lost for my rose," said the little prince, in order to remember.

"Men have forgotten this truth," said the fox. But you must not forget it. You become responsible forever for what you have tamed. You're responsible for your rose …

"I am responsible for my rose," repeated the little prince, in order to remember.

XXII

"Good morning," said the little prince.

"Good morning," said the switchman.

What are you doing here? Said the little prince.

"I'm sorting out the travelers, in bundles of a thousand," said the switchman. I ship the trains that take them, sometimes to the right, sometimes to the left. "

And a flashing light, thundering like a roar, made the switching cab tremble.

"They are in a great hurry," said the little prince. What are they looking for?

"The man of the locomotive ignores it himself," said the switchman.

And in a reverse direction, a second illuminated flash fell.

“They’re coming back already?” Asked the little prince.

“They are not the same,” said the switchman. It’s an exchange.

“They were not happy, where they were?”

“One is never satisfied where one is,” said the switchman.

And scolded the thunder of a third rapid illuminated.

“They are pursuing the first travelers. Asked the little prince.

“They are not pursuing anything at all,” said the switchman. They sleep in it, or they yawn. The children alone crush their noses against the windows.

“Children alone know what they are looking for,” said the little prince. They lose time for a rag doll, and it becomes very important, and if they are taken away, they cry …

“They’re lucky,” said the switchman.

XXIII

"Good morning," said the little prince.

"Good morning," said the merchant.

He was a merchant of sophisticated pills which appeased thirst. One swallows one a week, and one no longer feels the need to drink.

"Why do you sell that?" Said the little prince.

"It's a big saving of time," said the merchant. Experts have made calculations. We save fifty-three minutes a week.

"And what do we do for fifty-three minutes?" - We make what we want … "

"I," said the little prince, "if I had fifty-three minutes to spend, I would walk slowly towards a fountain."

XXIV

We were on the eighth day of my breakdown in the desert, and I had listened to the merchant's story, drinking the last drop of my supply of water:

"Ah! "I said to the little prince," they are very pretty, your memories, but I have not yet repaired my plane, I have nothing more to drink, and I should also be happy if I could walk gently towards a fountain!

"My friend, the fox," he said.

"My little fellow, it's no longer the fox!"

Why?

"Because we're going to die of thirst ..."

He did not understand my reasoning, but he replied:

"It's nice to have a friend, even if we're going to die. I am very glad to have had a friend fox ... "

"He does not measure danger," I said. He never has neither hunger nor thirst. A little sunlight is enough … »

But he looked at me and answered my thought:

"I'm thirsty too … look for a well …"

I made a gesture of weariness: it is absurd to look for a well, at random, in the immensity of the desert. Nevertheless, we set out on the march.

When we had walked for hours, in silence, night fell, and the stars began to light. I saw them as if in a dream, having a little fever, because of my thirst. The words of the little prince danced in my memory:

"Are you thirsty then, too?" I asked him.

But he did not answer my question. He simply says:

"Water can also be good for the heart …"

I did not understand his answer, but I was silent … I knew that he should not be interrogated.

He was tired. He sat. I sat down beside him. And after a pause he said, "The stars are beautiful, because of a flower that one does not see …"

I answered "of course" and I looked, without speaking, the folds of sand under the moon.

"The desert is beautiful," he added.

And it was true. I have always loved the desert. It sits on a sand dune. We see nothing. Nothing is heard. And yet something radiates in silence…

"What beautifies the desert," said the little prince, "is that he hides a well somewhere…"

I was surprised to suddenly understand this mysterious radiance of the sand. When I was a little boy I lived in an old house, and legend had it that a treasure was buried there. Of course, no one has ever discovered it, nor perhaps even sought it. But he delighted the whole house. My house hid a secret in the depths of her heart…

"Yes," said I to the little prince, "whether it be the house, the stars, or the desert, what makes their beauty invisible!

"I am satisfied," he said, "that you agree with my fox."

As the little prince fell asleep, I took him in my arms, and set off again. I was touched. It seemed to me to carry a fragile treasure. It even seemed to me that there was nothing more fragile on Earth. In the light of the moon, I looked at that pale brow, those closed eyes, the locks of hair that trembled in the wind, and I said to myself: "What I see here is only a bark. The most important is invisible … »

As his half-opened lips were half-smiling, I said to myself: "What moves me so strongly

about this little prince asleep is his fidelity to a flower, it is the image of a rose Radiates in him like the flame of a lamp, even when he sleeps … "And I guessed it even more fragile. It is necessary to protect the lamps: a gust of wind can extinguish them …

And, walking thus, I discovered the well at dawn.

XXV

"Men," said the little prince, "they go into the rapids, but they do not know what they are looking for." Then they move and turn in circles ...

And he added:

" It's not worth it... "

The well we reached did not resemble the Saharan wells. The Saharan wells are simple holes dug in the sand. This one resembled a village well. But there was no village there, and I thought I was dreaming.

"It's strange," I said to the little prince, "everything is ready: the pulley, the bucket and the rope ..."

He laughed, touched the rope, and pulled the pulley. And the pulley moaned as an old weathervane moaned when the wind had long slept.

"You hear," said the little prince, "we awaken this well and sings ..."

I did not want him to make an effort:

"Let me do it," I said, "it's too heavy for you. "

Slowly I hoisted the bucket up to the curb. I installed him there plumb. In my ears was the song of the pulley, and in the still trembling water I saw the sun shaking.

"I am thirsty for that water," said the little prince, "give me something to drink." And I understood what he had been looking for!

I lifted the bucket to her lips. He drank, his eyes closed. It was as sweet as a party. This water was much more than a food. It was born of the march under the stars, the song of the pulley, the effort of my arms. It was good for the heart, as a gift. When I was a little boy, the light of the Christmas tree, the music of the midnight mass, the sweetness of the smiles made all the radiance of the Christmas present that I received.

"The men of your house," said the little prince, "cultivate five thousand roses in the same garden, and they do not find what they seek."

"They do not find it," I replied.

And yet what they are looking for could be found in a single rose or a little water … "Of course," I replied.And the little prince added:

"But the eyes are blind. You must seek with your heart. "

I was drunk. I breathed well. The sand at daybreak is honey colored. I was also pleased with this color of honey. Why should I have trouble?

"You must keep your promise," said the little prince, who had once more sat down beside me.

"What promise?"

You know … a muzzle for my sheep … I am responsible for this flower! "

I took out my drawing sketches from my pocket. The little prince perceived them and said, laughing:

"Your baobabs, they look a bit like cabbages …"

Oh! "

I who was so proud of the baobabs!

"Your fox … his ears … they look a bit like horns … and they are too long! "

And he laughs again.

"You are unjust, little fellow, I knew nothing to draw but boas closed and boas open.

Oh! It will go, he said, the children know. "

So, I cracked a muzzle. And I had my heart tight and gave it to her:

"You have projects I do not know …"

But he did not answer me. He tells me:

"You know, my fall on Earth … tomorrow will be the anniversary…"

Then, after a pause, he said,

"I feel very close here…"

And he blushed.

And again, without understanding why, I experienced a bizarre grief. However, a question came to me:

“Then it was not by chance that the morning I met you a week ago, you walked like that, all alone, a thousand miles from all the inhabited regions! You were returning to the point of your fall? “

The little prince blushed again.

And I added, hesitating:

“Perhaps because of the birthday?”

The little prince blushed again. He never answered questions, but when you blush, it means “yes”, is not it?

“Ah! Said I, “I am afraid.”

But he answered:

“You have to work now. You have to go back to your machine. I’m waiting for you here. Come back tomorrow night … “

But I was not reassured. I remembered the fox. We risk crying a little if we let ourselves tame…

XXVI

There was, beside the well, a ruin of an old stone wall. When I returned from my work the next evening, I saw from afar my little prince sitting up there with his legs dangling. And I heard him speak:

"So, you do not remember?" he said. It's not quite here! "Another voice, no doubt, replied, for he replied," Yes! Yes! It's the day, but it's not here … "

I continued my walk towards the wall. I did not see or hear anyone. Yet the little prince replied again:

" … Of course. You will see where my trace begins in the sand. You just have to wait for me. I'll be there tonight. "

I was twenty meters from the wall, and I still could not see anything.

The little prince said again, after a silence:

"You have good venom?" Are you sure you will not

make me suffer for a long time?" I stopped, my heart tight, but I still did not understand. "Now go," he said, "I want to go down again!" "

Then I lowered my eyes to the foot of the wall, and I jumped! He was there, standing toward the little prince, one of those yellow snakes that execute you in thirty seconds. As I rummaged through my pocket to take out my revolver, I took the step, but at the noise I made, the serpent slowly sank into the sand, like a stream of water that dies, Pressing, slipped between the stones with a slight metallic sound. I reached the wall just in time to receive in my arms my little prince, pale as snow.

"What is that story?" You talk now with snakes! "

I had undone his eternal golden cowl. I had wet her temples and made her drink. And now I dared not ask him anything. He looked at me gravely and wrapped his arms around me. I felt his heartbeat like that of a bird that dies, when it has been shot with a rifle. He tells me:

"I'm glad you found what was missing from your machine. You can go home …

How do you know! "

I had just told him that, against all hope, I had succeeded in my work!

He did not answer my question, but he added:

"I too, today, go home …"

Attraction.jpg

Then, melancholy:

"It's much further … it's much harder …"

I felt that something extraordinary was happening. I held him in his arms like a little child, and yet it seemed to me that he was flowing vertically into an abyss without anything to restrain him.

He had a serious look, lost very far:

"I have your sheep. And I have the case for the sheep. And I have the muzzle … "

And he smiled with melancholy.

I waited a long time. I felt that it was getting warmer by degrees:

"Little fellow, you were afraid …"

He was afraid, of course! But he laughed softly:

"I'll be more afraid tonight …"

Again, I felt cold from the feeling of the irreparable. And I realized that I could not bear the idea of never hearing this laugh again. It was for me like a fountain in the desert.

"Little fellow, I still want to hear you laugh …"

But he said to me:

"Tonight, it will be a year. My star will be just above the place where I feel last year … "Little fellow, is it not a bad dream of a snake, a rendezvous, and a star?" But he did not answer my question. He tells me: "What's important is not seen …"

Of course…

It's like the flower. If you love a flower that is in

a star, it's sweet, at night, to look at the sky. All the stars are flourished.

Of course…

It's like water. The one you gave me to drink was like music, because of the pulley and the rope … you remember … it was good.

Of course…

You will watch at night, the stars. It's too small for me to show you where mine is. It's better like that. My star, it will be for you one of the stars. So, all the stars, you will love to look at them … They will be all your friends. And then I'll give you a present …"

He laughed again.

"Ah! Little fellow, little fellow, I like to hear this laughter!

It will be my gift … it will be like water …

What do you mean?

People have stars that are not the same. For some, who travel, the stars are guides. For others they are nothing but small lights. For others who are scholars they are problems. For my businessman they were gold. But all these stars are silent. You will have stars like no one has …

What do you mean?

“When you look at the sky at night, since I will live in one of them, since I will laugh in one of them, then it will be for you as if all the stars were laughing.” You will have stars that can laugh! “

And he laughs again.

“And when you are comforted (we always console ourselves) you will be glad to have known me. You will always be my friend. You’ll want to laugh with me. And sometimes you’ll open your window for fun … And your friends will be astonished to see you laughing at the sky. Then you will say to them: “Yes, the stars, it always makes me laugh!” And they will believe you crazy. I’ll have played you a nasty trick And he laughs again.

“It will be as if I had given you, instead of stars, lots of little bells that know how to laugh …”

And he laughs again. Then he became serious again:

“That night … you know … do not come.

I will not leave you.

"I shall look as if I am in pain. I shall look a little like die." It's like that. Do not come and see this, it's not worth it ...

I will not leave you. "But he was anxious.

"I tell you that ... it's because of the snake as well. He must not bite you ... Snakes are bad. It can bite for fun ...

I will not leave you.

But something reassured him:

"It's true they have no more venom for the second bite ..."

That night I did not see him set off. He had escaped quietly. When I succeeded in joining him, he walked resolutely, with a rapid step. He only said to me:

"Ah! you are the... "

And he took me by the hand. But he was still tormented:

" You were wrong. You'll have trouble. I shall look as if I am dead, and it will not be true."

I was silent.

" You understand. It is too far. I cannot carry that

body. It's too heavy. "I was silent.

"But it will be like an old, abandoned bark. It's not sad the old bark … "I was silent.

He was discouraged a little. But he made another effort:

"It'll be nice, you know. I too will look at the stars. All the stars will be wells with a rusty pulley. All the stars will pour me to drink … "

I was silent.

"It will be so much fun! You will have five hundred million bells; I will have five hundred million fountains … "

And he was silent too because he was crying …

" It's here. Let me step on my own. "And he sat down because he was afraid.

He says,

“You know … my flower … I am responsible! And she’s so weak! And she’s so naive. She has four thorns of nothing to protect her from the world … “

I sat down because I could not stand. He says:

”That’s it that’s all… “

He hesitated again a little, then he stood up. He took a step. I could not move.

There was nothing but a yellow flash near his ankle. He remained motionless for a moment. He did not shout. He fell Gently as a tree falls. It did not even make a noise, because of the sand.

Il tomba doucement comme tombe un arbre.

XXVII

And now, of course, it's been six years already … I've never told this story yet. The comrades who saw me were glad to see me alive again. I was sad but I said to them: "It's fatigue …"

Now I have comforted myself a little. That is … not quite. But I know that he has returned to his planet, for at daybreak I have not found his body. It was not such a heavy body … And I like the night listening to the stars. It's like five hundred million bells …

But now something extraordinary happens. The muzzle I designed for the little prince, I forgot to add the leather strap! He could never tie her to the sheep. So, I ask myself, "What happened on his planet?" Maybe the sheep ate the flower … "

Sometimes I say to myself: "Surely not! The little prince encloses his flower every night under his globe of glass, and he watches his sheep well. "Then I am happy. And all the stars laughed softly.

Sometimes I say to myself: "One is distracted once or the other, and that is enough! He forgot one evening the globe of glass, or else the sheep went out quietly during the night… "Then the bells changed into tears! …

This is a great mystery. For you who love the little prince as well as for me, nothing of the universe is alike if somewhere, one does not know where, a sheep that we do not know has, yes or no, eaten a rose …

Look at the sky. Ask yourself: "Did the sheep or not eat the flower? And you will see how everything changes …

And no big person will ever understand that it's so important!

This is for me, the most beautiful and saddest landscape in the world. It's the same landscape as the one on the previous page, but I drew it once more to show it to you. It is here that the little prince appeared on earth, then disappeared.

Look carefully at this landscape to be sure of recognizing it if you travel to Africa one day in the desert. And, if you happen to pass by there, I beseech you, do not hurry, wait a little right under the star! If a child comes to you, if he laughs, if he has golden hair, if he does not answer when asked, you will guess who he is. So be nice! Do not leave me so sad: write to me quickly that he has come back…

LIST OF TITLES WITH ISBN NO.

ISBN	TITLE
9788194914129	1984
9789390575220	1984 & Animal Farm (2In1)
9789390575572	1984 & Animal Farm (2In1): The International Best-Selling Classics
9789390575848	35 Sonnets
9789390575329	A Clergyman's Daughter
9789390575923	A Study In Scarlet
9789390896097	A Tale Of Two Cities
9789390896837	Abide in Christ
9789390896202	Abraham Lincoln
9789390896912	Absolute Surrender
9789390896608	African American Classic Collection
9789390575305	Aldous Huxley: The Collected Works
9789390896141	An Autobiography of M. K. Gandhi
9789390575886	Animal Farm
9789390575619	Animal Farm & The Great Gatsby (2In1)
9789390575626	Animal Farm & We
9789390896158	Anna Karenina
9789390575534	Antic Hay
9789390896165	Antony & Cleopatra
9789390896172	As I Lay Dying
9789390896226	As You like it
9789390575671	At Your Command
9789390575350	Awakened Imagination
9789390575114	Be What You Wish
9789390896233	Believe In yourself
9789390896998	Best of Charles Darwin: The Origin of Species & Autobiography
9789390896684	Best Of Horror : Dracula And Frankenstein
9789390575503	Best Of Mark Twain (The Adventures of Tom Sawyer AND The Adventures of Huckleberry Finn)
9789390896769	Black History Collection
9789390575756	Brave New World, Animal Farm & 1984 (3in1)

9789390896240	Brother Karamzov
9789390575053	Bulleh Shah Poetry
9789390575725	Burmese Days
9789390896257	Bushido
9789390896066	Can't Hurt Me
9788194914112	Chanakya Neeti: With The Complete Sutras
9789390896042	Crime and Punishment
9789390575527	Crome Yellow
9789390575046	Down and Out in Paris and London
9789390896844	Dracula
9789390575442	Emersons Essays: The Complete First & Second Series (Self-Reliance & Other Essays)
9789390575749	Emma
9789390575817	Essential Tozer Collection - The Pursuit of God & The Purpose of Man
9789390896578	Fascism What It Is and How to Fight It
9789390575688	Feeling is the Secret
9789390575190	Five Lessons
9789390575954	Frankenstein
9789390575237	Franz Kafka: Collected Works
9789390575282	Franz Kafka: Short Stories
9789390575060	George Orwell Collected Works
9789390575077	George Orwell Essays
9789390575213	George Orwell Poems
9788194914150	Greatest Poetry Ever Written Vol 1
9788194914143	Greatest Poetry Ever Written Vol 1
9789390896301	Gulliver's Travel
9789390575961	Gunaho Ka Devta
9789390575893	H. P. Lovecraft Selected Stories Vol 1
9789390575978	H. P. Lovecraft Selected Stories Vol 2
9789390896059	Hamlet
9789390575022	His Last Bow: Some Reminiscences of Sherlock Holmes
9789390896134	History of Western Philosophy
9789390575121	Homage To Catalonia

9789390896219	How to develop self-confidence and Improve public Speaking
9789390896295	How to enjoy your life and your Job
9789390575633	How to own your own mind
9789390896318	How to read Human Nature
9789390896325	How to sell your way through the life
9789390896370	How to use the laws of mind
9789390896387	How to use the power of prayer
9789390896028	How to win friends & Influence People
9788194824176	How To Win Friends and Influence People
9789390896103	Humility The Beauty of Holiness
9789390896653	Imperialism the Highest Stage of Capitalism
9789390575084	In Our Time
9789390575169	In Our Time & Three Stories and Ten poems
9789390575145	James Allen: The Collected Works
9789390896189	Jesus Himself
9789390575480	Jo's Boys
9789390896394	Julius Caesar
9789390575404	Keep the Aspidistra Flying
9789390896400	Kidnapped
9789390896424	King Lear
9789390575824	Lady Susan
9789390896455	Law of Success
9789390896264	Lincoln The Unknown
9789390575565	Little Men
9789390575640	Little Women
9788194914174	Lost Horizon
9789390896462	Macbeth
9789390896929	Man Eaters of Kumaon
9789390896523	Man The Dwelling Place of God
9789390896349	Man The Dwelling Place of God
9789390575909	Mansfield Park
9788194914136	Manto Ki 25 Sarvshreshth Kahaniya
9789390896509	Marxism, Anarchism, Communism
9789390575664	Mathematical Principles of Natural Philosophy

9788194914198	Meditations
9789390575800	Mein Kampf
9789390575794	Memory How To Develop, Train, And Use It
9789390896486	Mind Power
9789390896585	Money
9789390575039	Mortal Coils
9789390575770	My Life and Work
9789390896035	Narrative of the Life of Frederick Douglass
9789390575152	Neville Goddard: The Collected Works
9789390575985	Northanger Abbey
9789390896530	Notes From Underground
9789390896547	Oliver Twist
9789390575459	On War
9789390575541	One, None and a Hundred Thousand
9789390896554	Othelo
9789390575435	Out Of This World
9789390575015	Persuasion
9789390575510	Prayer The Art Of Believing
9789390575091	Pride and Prejudice
9789390896561	Psychic Perception
9789390575381	Rabindranath Tagore - 5 Best Short Stories Vol 2
9789390575367	Rabindranath Tagore - Short Stories (Masters Collections Including The Childs Return)
9789390575374	Rabindranath Tagore 5 Best Short Stories Vol 1 (Including The Childs Return
9789390896622	Romeo & Juliet
9789390896127	Sanatana Dharma
9789390575596	Seedtime & Harvest
9789390896639	Selected Stories of Guy De Maupassant
9789390575206	Self-Reliance & Other Essays
9789390575176	Sense and Sensibility
9789390575299	Shyamchi Aai
9789390896738	Socialism Utopian and Scientific
9789390896646	Success Through a Positive Mental Attitude
9789390575428	The Adventures of Huckleberry Finn

9789390575183	The Adventures of Sherlock Holmes
9789390575343	The Adventures of Tom Sawyer
9789390896691	The Alchemy Of Happiness
9789390575862	The Art Of Public Speaking
9789390896288	The Autobiography Of Charles Darwin
9788194914181	The Best of Franz Kafka: The Metamorphosis & The Trial
9789390575008	The Call Of Cthulhu and Other Weird Tales
9789390575107	The Case-Book of Sherlock Holmes
9789390896110	The Castle Of Otranto
9789390896745	The Communist Manifesto
9789390575589	The Complete Fiction of H. P. Lovecraft
9789390575497	The Complete Works of Florence Scovel Shinn
9789390896820	The Conquest of Breard
9789390896813	The Diary of a Young Girl
9789390896332	The Diary of a Young Girl The Definitive Edition of the Worlds Most Famous Diary
9789390575701	The Great Gatsby, Animal Farm & 1984 (3In1)
9789390575312	The Greatest Works Of George Orwell (5 Books) Including 1984 & Non-Fiction
9789390575992	The Hound of Baskervilles
9789390896707	The Idiot
9789390896714	The Invisible Man
9789390575657	The Knowledge of the holy
9789390575558	The Law & the Promise
9789390896721	The Law Of Attraction
9789390896776	The Leader in you
9789390896363	The Life of Christ
9789390896196	The Man-Eating Leopard of Rudraprayag
9789390896783	The Master Key to Riches
9789390575268	The Memoirs Of Sherlock Holmes
9789390896479	The Midsummer Night's Dream
9789390575466	The Mill On The Floss
9789390896790	The Miracles of your mind
9789390896660	The Mutual Aid A Factor in Evolution
9789390896448	The Origin of Species

9789390896905	The Peter Kropotkin Anthology The Conquest of Bread & Mutual Aid A Factor of Evolution
9789390896806	The Picture of Dorian Gray
9789390896271	The Picture of Dorian Gray
9789390575275	The Power Of Awareness
9789390896356	The Power of Concentration
9788194824169	The Power of Positive Thinking
9789390575411	The Power of the Spoken Word
9788194914105	The Power Of Your Subconscious Mind
9789390896899	The Power of Your Subconscious Mind
9789390896417	The Principles of Communism
9789390575787	The Psychology Of Mans Possible Evolution
9789390896615	The Psychology of Salesmanship
9789390575732	The Pursuit of God
9789390575398	The Pursuit of Happiness
9789390896851	The Quick and Easy Way to effective Speaking
9789390575947	The Return Of Sherlock Holmes
9789390575138	The Road To Wigan Pier
9789390896981	The Root of the Righteous
9789390575855	The Science Of Being Well
9788194914167	The Science Of Getting Rich, The Science Of Being Great & The Science Of Being Well (3In1)
9789390896011	The Screwtape Letters
9789390896073	The Screwtape Letters
9789390575336	The Secret Door to Success
9789390575695	The Secret Of Imagining
9789390896868	The Secret Of Success
9789390896431	The Seven Last Words
9789390575930	The Sign of the Four
9789390896004	The Sonnets
9789390896516	The Souls of Black Folk
9789390896875	The Sound and The Fury
9789390575244	The State and Revolution
9789390896882	The Story of My Life
9789390896936	The Story Of Oriental Philosophy

9789390896752	The Strange Case of Dr. Jekyll and Mr. Hyde
9789390896943	The Tempest
9789390575916	The Valley Of Fear
9789390575879	The Wind in the willows
9789390896080	The Wind in the willows
9789390575763	Their eyes were watching gofd
9789390575831	Three Stories
9789390896950	Twelfth Night
9789390896592	Twelve Years a Slave
9789390896677	Up from Slavery
9789390896974	Value Price and Profit
9789390896967	Wake Up and Live
9789390896493	With Christ in the School of Prayer
9789390575602	Your Faith is Your Fortune
9789390575473	Your Infinite Power To Be Rich
9789390575251	Your Word is Your Wand
9789390575718	Youth
9789391316099	A Christmas Carol
9789391316105	A Doll's House
9789391316501	A Passage to India
9789391316709	A Portrait of the Artist as a Young Man
9789391316112	A Tale of Two Cities
9789391316747	A Tear and a Smile
9789391316167	Agnes Gray
9789391316174	Alice's Adventures in Wonderland
9789391316136	Anandamath
9789391316181	Anne Of Green Gables
9789391316754	Anthem
9789391316198	Around The World in 80 Days
9789391316013	As A Man Thinketh
9789391316242	Autobiography of a Yogi
9789391316266	Beyond Good and Evil
9789391316761	Bleak House
9789391316778	Chitra, a Play in One Act
9789391316310	David Copperfield

9789391316075	Demian
9789391316785	Dubliners
9789391316051	Favourite Tales from the Arabian Nights
9789391316235	Gitanjali
9789391316068	Gravity
9789391316150	Great Speeches of Abraham Lincoln
9789391316662	Guerilla Warfare
9789391316839	Kim
9789391316822	Mother
9789391316211	My Childhood
9789391316846	Nationalism
9789391316327	Oliver Twist
9789391316853	Pygmalion
9789391316334	Relativity: The Special and the General Theory
9789391316389	Scientific Healing Affirmation
9789391316341	Sons and Lovers
9789391316587	Tales from India
9789391316372	Tess of The D'Urbervilles
9789391316396	The Awakening and Selected Stories
9789391316402	The Bhagvad Gita
9789391316303	The Book of Enoch
9789391316228	The Canterville Ghost
9789391316907	The Dynamic Laws of Prosperity
9789391316006	The Great Gatsby
9789391316860	The Hungry Stones and Other Stories
9789391316433	The Idiot
9789391316440	The Importance of Being Earnest
9789391316297	The Light of Asia
9789391316914	The Madman His Parables and Poems
9789391316457	The Odyssey
9789391316921	The Picture of Dorian Gray
9789391316464	The Prince
9789391316938	The Prophet
9789391316945	The Republic
9789391316518	The Scarlet Letter

9789391316143	The Seven Laws of Teaching
9789391316525	The Story of My Experiments with Truth
9789391316532	The Tales of the Mother Goose
9789391316549	The Thirty Nine Steps
9789391316594	The Time Machine
9789391316600	The Turn of the Screw
9789391316983	The Upanishads
9789391316617	The Yellow Wallpaper
9789391316426	The Yoga Sutras of Patanjali
9789391316990	Ulysses
9789391316624	Utopia
9789391316679	Vanity Fair
9789391316020	What Is To Be Done
9789391316686	Within A Budding Grove
9789391316693	Women in Love